Scrambled Eggs and Spider Legs

Scrambled Eggs and Spider Legs

BY GARY HOGG

ILLUSTRATED BY GREGG THORKELSON

A
LITTLE APPLE
PAPERBACK

SCHOLASTIC INC.

New York   Toronto   London   Auckland   Sydney

ISBN 0-590-20589-7

12 11 10 9 8 7   2 3/0

Printed in the U.S.A.   40
First Scholastic printing, April 1998

for Verda Rae,
a truly wonderful person.

CONTENTS

1

The Burp Heard Around the School

"Good morning, Taters," boomed Mr. Abrams's voice over the intercom. "It's another *spudtacular* day here at Dayton Elementary. Today the morning announcements will be read by Matt Daring from Mr. Broadhead's second-grade class."

Matt was nervous. Soon the entire school would be listening to his every word. Putting his mouth right next to the microphone, he tried to remember all of the advice he had been given.

"Speak loudly," said his teacher, Mr. Broadhead.

"Say your words clearly," said Mrs. Johnson, the secretary.

"Don't talk too fast," advised Ms. Walker, the librarian.

"I'll give you a buck to burp into the microphone," said his best friend, Roger.

Matt decided to take Roger's advice. He took a big gulp of air and let it rip. The speaker system turned Matt's burp into a huge monster belch.

The megablast shocked everyone. Mrs. McDonald, the school cook, dropped a tray full of dishes. Ms. Wagner's class thought it was an earthquake and got under their desks. Mr. Jordan, the P.E. teacher, almost swallowed his whistle.

Matt looked over at the principal. Mr.

Abrams was biting his lip, and his face was turning bright red.

Oh no, thought Matt. I'm dead meat. Thinking quickly, he put his lips next to the microphone a second time. "Ex-cu-u-u-u-u-se me! Guess I had too many Cheerios for breakfast," he explained.

Mr. Abrams let out a big sigh of relief. The burp that almost destroyed the school had been an accident.

The rest of the announcements went smoothly. Matt spoke loudly, clearly, and slowly.

When he had read off the last item, Matt turned to Mr. Abrams. "I'm sorry about the burp," he apologized.

"That's okay," said Mr. Abrams, patting Matt on the head. "You did a fine job. Now hurry back to class."

As Matt left the office, he heard Mr. Abrams tell Mrs. Johnson, "Get the custodian in here quick. Tell him to bring his strongest cleaner. I want that microphone sterilized."

Matt hurried down the hall. He wanted to get his dollar while the burp was still fresh in Roger's mind. Entering the classroom, Matt looked right at his best friend. Roger gave Matt a thumbs-up and slid a wadded-up dollar to the corner of his desk.

Matt headed straight for Roger's desk. He grabbed the dollar and kept going. When he slid into his seat, Mr. Broadhead started talking.

"Nice job, Matthew. Other than the rough beginning, you made the entire class proud."

Matt smiled. Mission accomplished. He burped, got the money, and lived to tell about it.

2

It's Raining Money

The morning seemed to zip by. Matt spent most of the time dreaming about what to buy with his dollar. It was a short list: candy, candy, and more candy. Matt's sweet dreams were interrupted by the morning recess bell.

After Matt and Roger left the classroom, they headed straight for the monkey bars. Roger was dying to win his money back from Matt.

"I'll bet you a dollar I can hang upside down longer than you can," said Roger.

"You're on," said Matt, climbing up the side of the monkey bars. Soon, Matt and his best friend were hanging upside down like a couple of second-grade bats.

Suddenly, Ryan Burk came racing toward the monkey bars. With a flying leap, he grabbed one of the high bars and swung himself up next to Matt.

"Don't make a sound," whispered Ryan. "He's after me."

"Who?" asked Matt.

"Nick Dudley," whispered Ryan. "He's the world's meanest bully, and he wants to cream me."

"What did you do?" asked Matt.

"Nothing," replied Ryan. "He just hates second-graders. Shhh, there he is."

Nick was a huge boy. His hair was short and greased back.

"Okay, you little creep, where did you go?" growled Nick as he got to the monkey bars. The boys were silent as Nick stood right below them. The seconds ticked by. Nick was about to leave when Matt's dollar fell out of his pocket and floated down to the ground. It landed right next to Nick's shoes.

"Hey, it's raining money," said Nick, grabbing the money.

"That's my dollar!" called out Matt.

Nick laughed and looked at the dollar. "I don't see your name on it, unless you're George Washington."

"It fell out of my pocket," said Matt. "Can I please have it back?"

"Can I please have it back," said Nick, trying to sound like a baby. He let out a huge laugh. "Sometimes I really crack myself up."

Matt grabbed the bar in front of him and came swinging off the monkey bars.

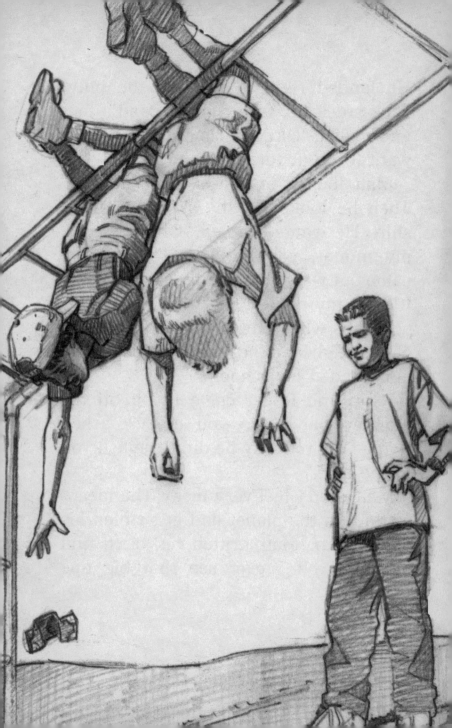

He landed right in front of the bully. Nick stuck his face right in Matt's face and yelled, "Okay, shrimp, what do you want to do about it?"

Matt looked at Nick's clenched fists. Then he looked at the skull on Nick's shirt. He wanted to yell, "Give me back my money, you big creep!" But what came out was, "I guess I made a mistake. It's not my money."

"That's what I thought you'd say," said Nick. He shoved the money in his pocket and headed for school.

Ryan and Roger came flying off the monkey bars. "Are you crazy?" asked Ryan. "You're lucky he didn't smash you in the face."

Matt didn't feel very lucky. The meanest kid on the planet had just stolen his only dollar. Matt gritted his teeth and mumbled, "If I ever see that big ape again, I'm going to teach him a thing or two."

"The only thing you could teach him is how to stop the bleeding after he punches you in the nose," said Roger, laughing.

"Very funny," said Matt as the boys headed back to class. "You'll see, I'll get him."

3
Spud Dud

Matt was still fuming over his lost money when Mr. Broadhead called the class to attention. "Students, today is the day we meet our Spud Buds."

Roger's hand shot up. "What's a Spud Bud?" he asked.

"Mrs. Pullman's fifth-grade students are going to be our helpers this year," said Mr. Broadhead. "Each one of you will be assigned a partner from her class. Since we are the Dayton Taters, your helper will be called your Spud Bud.

"You and your partner will work on lots of different projects during the year. You'll write stories, create art projects, and even act in a play together."

"This sounds like fun," said Melanie.

"Oh, it is," Mr. Broadhead said. "Now, clean off your desks because Mrs. Pull-man and her class will be here any minute."

Matt was sliding his spelling book into his desk when the classroom door opened. When he looked up, he couldn't believe his eyes. The first fifth-grader through the door was the bully, Nick Dudley.

"Oh no," moaned Matt.

Nick was followed by the rest of Mrs.

Pullman's class. Each student was carrying a chair. They lined up against the wall at the front of the room.

When Roger spotted Nick, he leaned over and whispered to Matt, "Are you going to teach him a thing or two now or wait until he gets you in a headlock?"

Mr. Broadhead spoke up, "Class, I want to introduce you to some of the best fifth-graders in the world."

Mrs. Pullman's students burst into smiles. A couple of them clasped their hands over their heads. Nick just grunted and stared at the floor. He'd rather eat dirt than stand in front of a bunch of silly second-graders.

"Boys and girls, I've been looking forward to this day," said Mrs. Pullman. "We think we have chosen each of you a partner whom you will really like. As Mr. Broadhead calls your name, please stand up. Your Spud Bud will come over and sit down next to you."

Matt slumped down in his chair. He got out his lucky baseball card and started rubbing it. "Anyone but Nick," he said over and over.

Mr. Broadhead quickly read the names. The fifth-graders were very cheerful as they went over to their Spud Buds. Each of them gave their second-grade buddy a high five.

Matt was still rubbing his lucky baseball card when Mr. Broadhead called his name. He stood up and looked at the remaining fifth-graders, Nick, Raymond, and Missy.

When Missy started to move, Matt let out a sigh of relief. Even a girl would be better than Nick. Missy took two steps and stopped. She picked up her pencil and moved back into line.

Nick gave his chair a big shove, and it slid down the row toward Matt. Nick slowly followed the chair. His feet were barely moving as he shuffled across the floor.

"Mr. Dudley," said Mrs. Pullman, "we don't have all day."

Nick picked up the pace and stopped next to Matt. Matt reluctantly held his hand up for a high five. Instead of a high five, Nick punched Matt in the arm and said, "Well, if it isn't George Washington."

Matt tore up his lucky baseball card and shoved it in his pocket. Everyone in the class got a Spud Bud, and he ended up with a Spud Dud.

4

No Comment

"Listen, you little goofball," snapped Nick. "I think this whole idea is stupid. You better not expect me to do one stinking thing to help you. Do you understand?"

"I get the picture," mumbled Matt.

"I can see from the looks on your faces that we did a great job of pairing you up," said Mr. Broadhead. "Your first assignment is to interview your Spud Bud.

Pretend that you are a newspaper reporter. Find out all you can about your partner, and then write a newspaper article featuring your helper."

"Oh great," moaned Matt. He got out his notebook and looked over at Nick, who was busy drawing a snake's head on his hand with a black pen.

"Go ahead," said Nick. "Ask me some dumb questions."

"How old are you?" asked Matt.

"No comment," replied Nick.

"What's your favorite food?" asked Matt.

"No comment," answered Nick. "That's classified information. Now, I'll save you some time. The answers to your next four questions are 'No comment. No comment. No comment' and 'NO COMMENT!' "

Matt slowly shut his notebook, and Nick went back to work on the snake's head. They were quiet for the rest of Spud Bud time.

At lunch, Matt got his lunch tray and hurried over to Roger. Roger always brought cold lunch from home. He was almost done with his sandwich when Matt sat down.

"So, how was your interview with Mr. Mean?" asked Roger.

"It was about as interesting as interviewing the peanut butter in your sandwich," said Matt. "Nick said 'no comment' to every question."

"Wow," said Roger. "How did your newspaper article turn out?"

"It just says that Nick is a fifth-grader and he likes snakes," said Matt.

"That's all you could come up with?" asked Roger.

"Well, I couldn't write down what a creep I think he is," said Matt.

"Sure you could," said Roger. "Extra!

Extra! Read all about it. Nick Dudley is the biggest jerk on earth." Both boys started to laugh.

"Hurry and finish your lunch," said Roger. "I'll go and get some paper. We'll meet by the monkey bars and write an article about the real Nick Dudley."

Matt and Roger spent the rest of lunch writing down mean things about Nick. Their newspaper article made Godzilla look like a pussycat compared to Nick. When they were done, Matt said, "We really let that big bully have it. The part about his breath smelling worse than dead worms is my favorite."

The boys went straight to the big green file cabinet when they got back to their classroom. Each student in Mr. Broadhead's class had a section of the cabinet where their finished work was kept. Matt took out his writing folder and placed the new article in it.

"If Nick ever reads that article, he'll be furious," said Roger.

"You know what they say, the truth hurts," replied Matt.

"Yeah, but you'll be the one hurting after Nick gets through with you," said Roger.

"Don't worry," said Matt. "The only article Nick will ever see is the short and sweet one."

Matt hurried to his seat when Mr. Broadhead walked into the room. Matt took out his spelling word list and read through the words. There wasn't another Spud Bud time until Thursday, and he wasn't going to think about Nick again until then.

5
Rude Dude

Thursday afternoon was just like any other day until the door opened and in marched Mrs. Pullman's class.

"It's Spud Bud time," called out Mr. Broadhead.

Matt watched as the fifth-graders lined up at the front of the room. When he didn't see Nick, he let out a big sigh of relief. Nick must be home sick or in Mr. Abrams's office.

Matt was relaxing in his chair when he heard someone in the hall yell, "I didn't do it!" The door flew open, and in stomped Nick. He was followed by Mrs. Pullman. She looked very upset.

"Is everything all right?" asked Mr. Broadhead.

"It is now," replied Mrs. Pullman.

Mr. Broadhead walked over to the green file cabinet and got out the second-graders' writing folders. "Class, today is the day we share the newspaper articles we wrote about our Spud Buds," he said. "Your Spud Bud will read your article out loud."

Matt was watching Mr. Broadhead pass out the folders when he suddenly remembered the second article. He couldn't let Nick get his hands on it.

Matt threw his arm in the air so hard and fast, it almost rocketed off his body. "Mr. Broadhead, can I please have my folder for a second? I need to make a change or two in my article."

"We don't have time for making changes," said Mr. Broadhead.

Matt sunk as low as he could without actually being on the floor. He didn't even listen as the other students read. He was too busy crossing his fingers and hoping that Nick would not see the second newspaper article.

As usual, Nick was the last student in line. He leaned against Mr. Broadhead's desk and cleared his throat. Matt closed his eyes as Nick started to read.

"Nick Dudley is . . ." Nick stopped and cleared his throat again. Then there was a long pause.

Matt opened one eye a crack to see what was going on. Nick was just standing there staring at the paper. Finally, he started again, "Nick Dudley is a fifth-grader and he likes snakes. The end."

A huge sigh of relief flowed out of Matt. "I am Mr. Lucky," he whispered to himself.

Up in front of the class, Mr. Broadhead began to describe the students' next project. "Your assignment is to write Tater Tales," explained Mr. Broadhead. "You can write a mystery, an adventure, a sports story, or even a love story. The most important thing is that your story must involve potatoes. We'll begin work on the stories the next time we meet."

As Mrs. Pullman's class began to file out, Nick made a detour over to Matt. He dropped a piece of paper onto the desk and said, "You are mashed potatoes, rude dude."

Matt looked down and saw the second article. He felt the blood drain from his face and his knees start knocking. It looked as if Mr. Lucky was going to be introduced to Mr. Mean's fists.

6

Sweating Bullets

For the rest of the afternoon, Matt looked like an ostrich with his head buried in his desk. When the bell rang to go home, Matt started sweating bullets. He was sure Nick would be waiting for him.

Luckily, it was Thursday. Matt's mother would be picking him up after school. If he could just make it to the car, he'd be safe.

The classroom was empty except for Matt and Mr. Broadhead. Mr. Broadhead cleared his throat loudly. He was trying politely to give Matt a hint to move on.

Matt searched his desk for anything he might be able to use as a weapon. If Nick attacked him, he at least wanted to be armed. Grabbing a purple crayon and a bottle of glue, Matt got up from his desk. He popped his head out of the doorway and looked up and down the hall. Everything was very quiet.

Matt entered the hallway like a spy. As he shuffled along slowly, his keen eyes searched every doorway and garbage can. Nick could be hiding anywhere.

Suddenly, Matt heard a shuffling sound behind him. He froze in his tracks. He was sure that it was Nick. Spinning around like a ninja, Matt flew into action. The purple crayon was a blur as he whipped it back and forth. Jabbing the bottle of glue at his enemy, he prepared to squirt.

There stood Mr. Reynolds, the custodian. "Hold it, young man. You wouldn't squirt glue at an unarmed man, would you?"

Matt began to relax. "I'm sorry," he said. "I thought you were someone else."

"I'd hate to be in his shoes," Mr. Reynolds laughed. "He's going to be purple and sticky when you get through with him."

Matt hurried to the front door of the school and then stopped. He still had to make it to the car without bumping into Nick.

Stepping into the bright sunlight, Matt spotted his mom's car and took off running. Bobbing and weaving from the flagpole to the bike rack, he finally made it to the parking lot.

Jerking the car door open, Matt

slammed his body into the front seat. He immediately locked the door.

"Burn rubber, Mom!" he snapped. "We've got to get out of here!"

"We'll leave soon enough," Mrs. Daring said calmly. "First, I want you to meet someone. His name is Nick. His mother and I play golf together. He needs a ride home, so we're giving him a lift."

Matt's bottom seemed stuck to the seat. Only his head moved as he slowly looked around. Sitting in the backseat was Nick. He was smiling like the cat that had just eaten the canary.

"Hi, Spud Bud." Nick laughed. "Long time no see."

"Do you two know each other?" asked Mrs. Daring.

"We're buddies," said Nick. "We're writing a Tater Tale together for school. I was hoping you could drop off Matt at my house so we could work on our story."

Matt gulped. "I can't. I have to get home," he insisted. Matt's voice was high and squeaky.

Mrs. Daring totally ignored her son. "I think that's a lovely idea. You boys can work together while I run some errands."

The ride to Nick's house was intense. Matt kept squirming like a worm on a fishing trip.

"What's your story going to be about?" asked Mrs. Daring.

"It's going to have a lot of fighting in it," said Nick excitedly. "I figure we'll have this big mean potato beat this little potato to smithereens."

"Oh, that sounds a little rough," said Mrs. Daring as she turned the car onto Washington Street.

Finally, they pulled up in front of a yellow house. Nick jumped out and waited for Matt.

"Please, Mom, I want to stay with you," pleaded Matt.

His mother was about to agree, when Nick opened the car door and grabbed Matt by the arm. "Come on, Spud Bud, we have a lot of work to do."

He dragged Matt out of the car. "Don't worry about Matt, I'll take good care of him," said Nick as he slammed the door.

Matt felt a lump the size of Texas form in his throat as his mother drove away.

7

Itsy-bitsy Spider

Nick was smiling like an angel as he waved good-bye to Mrs. Daring. But when he looked at Matt, his smile faded.

"I think we have a score to settle," growled Nick.

"You can have everything I've got," offered Matt, emptying his pockets. There was the purple crayon, some chewed gum wrapped in paper, the bottle of glue, and a rusty key.

"I don't need any of that junk," snapped Nick. "What I need is a servant."

"I can't be your serv —" But before Matt could finish, Nick held up both of his fists.

"I'd love to be your servant," added Matt quickly.

"Good," said Nick, rubbing his hands together. "First I want you to wash my bike, and then you can clean up the back-yard."

Nick's bike was a wreck. The padding was torn off the seat, and the front tire was almost flat. Matt scrubbed off as much dirt as he could. He thought the bike still looked crummy, but Nick was pleased.

"Good work, servant boy," said Nick. "Now, get to work on the yard."

As they walked around to the back of the house, Matt couldn't believe his eyes. It looked more like a junkyard than a backyard. This was a job for the marines, not a second-grader.

"Well, what are you waiting for?" yelled Nick. "Get to work, or I'll work *you* over."

Matt picked up a rusty old pipe and headed for the garbage can.

"What do you think you're doing?" shouted Nick. "That's a perfectly good telescope."

Matt held the heavy pipe up to his eye and looked into it. "I can't see anything," he said.

"You doofus," said Nick, laughing. "You have to pound the dirt out of it first." He grabbed the pipe and began banging it on the ground. Nick shook out some dust and clods and held it up to his eye.

"I can see the whole world through this," he announced. The rusty pipe left a brown circle around Nick's left eye.

"Now, don't try to throw away any other cool stuff."

Matt looked around the yard and wondered what junk was cool stuff and what junk was garbage. He spotted a stack of old newspapers and picked them up. He hauled them over and tossed them into the garbage can.

"That's enough cleaning for today," announced Nick. "I feel like a backwards bear hunt."

"What's a backwards bear hunt?" asked Matt.

"It's backwards because the bear does the hunting," said Nick. "I'm the bear, and I'm going to hunt you. Just to make it fair, I'll give you a head start. I'll count to ten, and then I'll attack."

Matt took off as fast as he could. He had gone just a couple of feet when Nick came after him. "You said you were going to count to ten!" yelled Matt.

"You idiot, bears can't count," said Nick, laughing.

Matt headed for the biggest tree in the yard. He grabbed the first branch and climbed like he had never climbed before. He was high in the tree in no time.

Nick got to the trunk and stopped. Looking up at Matt, he said, "It looks like there's a nut in this tree, and bears love to eat nuts." He let out a loud growl and started to climb.

Matt grabbed a small branch and broke it off. He knew it wouldn't stop Nick, but it was worth a try. Matt pointed the stick at Nick and said, "Back off, or I'll poke you."

Nick laughed and was reaching up to grab the stick when he suddenly stopped. His eyes grew big, and he started racing down the tree. "Get that spider away from me!" yelled Nick.

Matt looked at the end of the stick and saw a medium-sized black spider that was harmless and holding on for dear life.

Nick was almost to the ground when he slipped and fell out of the tree. He landed on his back, looking right up at Matt.

Matt gave the stick a little shake, and the spider came loose. The spider's web acted like a parachute. The miniature paratrooper slowly floated down and landed on Nick's face.

Nick went berserk. He jumped up and began running around the yard. He threw himself back on the ground and flipped around like a fish out of water.

Matt just stared. He couldn't believe it. Big bad Nick was scared to death of spiders.

The sound of Matt's mom honking the

car horn brought Nick back to his senses.

"I've got to go," said Matt.

"You can go, but remember, you're still my servant," said Nick, getting up off the ground. "And don't tell anyone, or you know what will happen."

"Okay, Spiderman," teased Matt as he ran to the front of the house.

8

Scrambled Stomach

The bell for lunchtime used to be Matt's second favorite sound of the day. The bell to go home was his favorite. But now lunch was just one more time he risked running into Nick.

At the sound of the bell, Roger jumped up from his desk and grabbed his lunch box. "Come on, Matt, my mom packed extra cookies today. I'll split them with you," he said, heading for the door.

The thought of having one of Roger's mom's chocolate chip cookies gave Matt the courage he needed to head for the lunchroom.

By the time Matt got his hot lunch, Roger was already munching on a sandwich. "How do you like your Spud Bud?" asked Roger.

"Terrible," said Matt. "He thinks I'm his servant."

"That stinks," said Roger.

Suddenly, Matt scampered under the table.

"What's going on?" asked Roger. Roger didn't get a chance to see. Someone had his hands firmly over his eyes.

"Hey, what's the big idea?" demanded Roger, squirming to get loose.

"Guess who?" came the reply.

Roger immediately recognized Nick's voice. Nick pushed his fingers into Roger's eyes extra hard and then let go.

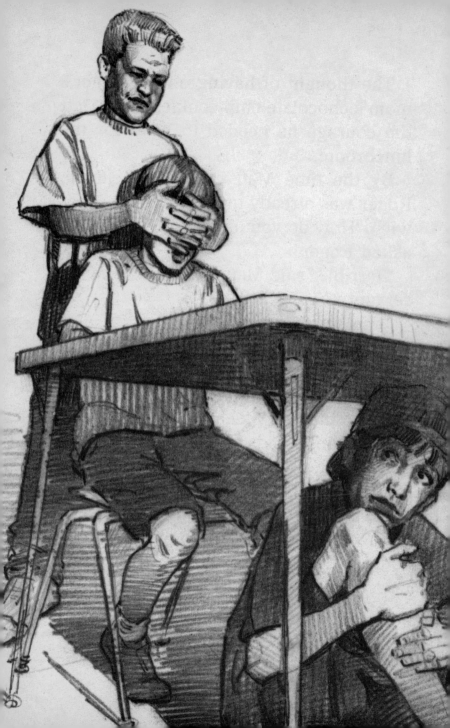

"Have you seen my servant?" asked Nick.

"You mean Matt?" asked Roger. "I haven't seen him all day. I think he's home sick."

"Then who does this lunch tray belong to?" demanded Nick.

"It's mine," replied Roger.

"You eat two lunches?" asked Nick.

"You bet. I'm a growing boy," answered Roger.

"Good," said Nick, grabbing Roger's sandwich. "Those fish sticks they served today tasted like garbage. I could only eat mine and the six I stole from those third-graders. I'm still starving."

Nick took one giant bite out of Roger's sandwich. He started to chew, and then his mouth froze. He quickly opened the bread slices to see what was in the sandwich. Immediately, he spit the mouthful of chewed sandwich into Roger's lunch box.

"There're greasy scrambled eggs in that stinking sandwich," said Nick, gagging.

"Cold scrambled egg sandwiches are my favorite," said Roger proudly.

Nick sat down on the bench and started rubbing his belly. "Scrambled eggs are the grossest food on earth," he groaned. "I get an upset stomach every time I get near them. What kind of sicko would put them in a sandwich?"

"We eat them all the time," said Roger.

Nick didn't hear Roger. He was making a fast dash for the rest room. The scrambled eggs had scrambled Nick's stomach, and he wasn't feeling so well.

"I'll tell Matt you said 'hello,' " said Roger, laughing as Nick ran away.

Matt poked his head out from under

the bench. "What did you do to make Nick take off like that?" he asked.

"I guess Nick's not a real egg lover," laughed Roger. "My scrambled egg sandwich made him sick."

Matt climbed back onto the bench. "Do you have another one?" asked Matt. "I could use it when we meet with our Spud Buds this afternoon."

"Sorry," Roger said. "I'm fresh out."

9

Scary Harry

When the two classes met that afternoon, Nick had recovered from the sandwich and was as mean as ever. He plopped his chair down next to Matt's and threw a stack of homework papers on Matt's desk.

"You can work on the stupid potato story later," snapped Nick. "Now I want you to do this homework for me."

Matt's eyes grew big. "I can't do this

work. I'm only a second-grader, and these are fifth-grade problems."

"You can do them as good as I can." Nick laughed. "Now, get to work, or you'll get to see what a mashed potato feels like."

Matt squinted as he tried to read the first math problem. He didn't have a clue what it was about. Finally, he just wrote down 49 as the answer.

"How's it coming?" grunted Nick.

"It's easier than I thought," said Matt, writing 49 as the answer to every single problem.

Mr. Broadhead called the students to attention. "I hope your Tater Tales are coming along nicely. Tomorrow when we meet, we will share them. Both members of your team will need to help present the story. Take the next few minutes and decide how you want to do that."

Nick put his face close to Matt's.

"Okay, George Washington, you better write a great story for us. And plan on reading it yourself. I'm not reading anything in front of these goofballs."

"But — but Mr. Broadhead said . . ." stuttered Matt.

"I don't care what Mr. Potatohead said, I'm not reading," insisted Nick.

As soon as Matt got home, he went to his room and started to work on the potato story. He stared at the ceiling. He stared at the floor. He closed his eyes so tight he could see stars, but he couldn't come up with an idea. His mind was as blank as the paper.

Finally, he wrote, "I hate Nick's guts. The end." Matt threw his pencil down and went to feed his pets.

Gil was Matt's goldfish. Matt put a pinch of fish food between his fingers and rubbed them together over the fishbowl. The food sprinkled evenly into the water. Gil attacked the food as if he were a shark.

Matt called out, "Hey, Hermie, are you hungry?" Hermie was Matt's pet hamster. The sound of Matt's voice excited the hamster, and he ran around the cage.

"That's my boy," said Matt, filling Hermie's dish with food.

Matt moved to the terrarium sitting on the ledge by the window. It was a large glass box and the home for Harry the tarantula. He was scary-looking but very friendly. Matt stuck his arm in the terrarium, and the giant spider climbed onto his hand. Harry scurried up to Matt's shoulder.

Looking over at Harry, Matt said, "Hi, buddy, how do a couple of fat bugs sound for dinner? There's a really big bug at school I would love to feed to you.

His name is Nick. On second thought, he probably wouldn't taste very good. He's pretty rotten."

Matt put his hand on his desk, and Harry crawled down his arm onto the notebook. Watching Harry gave Matt a great idea. He quickly put Harry back in the terrarium and grabbed his pencil. He went back to work on the story. This time the words flew onto the paper.

10

Tater Time

Matt was up early the next morning. He had to get things ready for school. "Mom, can I bring lunch to school today?" he called out.

"Sure," replied Mrs. Daring. "How about a tuna fish sandwich?"

"Actually," said Matt, "I've been craving a scrambled egg sandwich. Roger eats them all the time, and he says they're great."

"Sounds awful to me," Matt's mother

said. "But if that's what you want, I'll make it."

When Matt entered the kitchen, he had his backpack on and was ready to go. He grabbed his lunch and headed for the door.

"Just a minute, young man," said Mrs. Daring. "Aren't you forgetting something?"

"Oh, yeah," said Matt. He rushed over and gave his mom a kiss on the cheek.

"Your backpack looks very full today," Mrs. Daring said. "What do you have in it?"

"It's just a bunch of stuff I need for my potato story," said Matt as he dashed out the door.

After the morning announcements, Mr. Broadhead let the students have some time to put the finishing touches on their Tater Tales. Roger and Matt met at the pencil sharpener.

"Nick was looking for you before school this morning," said Roger, turning the handle of the sharpener. "He said he had some work for you to do."

"He can do it himself," stated Matt. "I'm through being a servant for Mr. Mean."

"That kind of talk could get you beat up," warned Roger.

"I think I know how to put Nick the Bully in his place," said Matt.

"I hope so," said Roger. "If not, he'll put you in your place. And that place will be the hospital."

The boys finished sharpening their pencils and returned to their seats. During recess and lunch, Matt kept out of sight as much as possible. He didn't want to see Nick until Spud Bud time.

When the fifth-graders arrived at Mr. Broadhead's classroom, Nick was the first one to enter. He marched right over to Matt and punched him on the arm.

"You little twerp. I missed every one of those math problems you did for me."

"Sorry," said Matt, rubbing his arm.

"Our story better be good or I'll punch more than that stick you call an arm," warned Nick.

"I wrote a great story," bragged Matt. "It's called 'Frankenspud,' and you won't have to read a word."

"Good," snapped Nick.

"All you have to do is walk around like Frankenstein's monster. Can you do that?" asked Matt.

"I'll do better than that. I'll grunt while I walk. I'm a good grunter," bragged Nick.

"Okay, but not too loud," replied Matt.

Matt was nervous as the students read their Tater Tales. Most of the stories were great.

Nolan Palmer and his partner wrote a sports story. It was about a spudball game between the Pittsburgh Peelers and the Oakland Raider Taters.

Tiffany Cox and her Spud Bud wrote a mystery. It was called "Something's Rotten in Mashville."

Missy and Roger's story told about a beautiful potato princess who lived in a casserole.

After Roger's story, Nick leaned over and whispered to Matt, "Our story better be better than that one. And you better not have put any princesses or sissy junk in it."

"Stop worrying," Matt said. "Our story will have the class on the edge of their seats."

11

"Frankenspud"

At last it was Nick and Matt's turn. Matt grabbed his backpack, and the boys walked to the front of the room.

Matt cleared his throat and began to speak: "Our Tater Tale is called 'Frankenspud.'

"In the olden days, there was a mean monster. His name was Frankenspud."

Nick started walking around with stiff

legs. His arms were straight out, and he was grunting up a storm.

"Frankenspud made all the little tater tots of Spudville be his servants. If they didn't do what he told them, he would mash them. Every day the little tater tots cried big tater tears."

Nick put his hands together and shook them above his head. He was smiling. So far, he really liked the story.

"One sunny day, the potato circus came to Spudville. It was a great show.

"The French Fry Brothers from France did death-defying flips into pools of fry sauce.

"Hash Brown the Clown was hilarious. He even hit himself in the face with a sour-cream pie.

"Potato Patty was the queen of the tater trapeze. She swung on long vines high above the crowd.

"The circus had the strongest spud in the world. His name was Arnold Schwarzentater. His potato power was awesome.

"Reggie the Veggie and his Spud Spiders were the scariest. When Reggie brought out his taterantula everyone screamed."

Nick stopped smiling. He didn't like any story that had spiders in it.

"Tom Tater was one of Frankenspud's servants. He snuck off to the circus. He told everyone about mean Frankenspud. Arnold Schwarzentater got so mad, his potato eyes bugged out.

"Tom led all of the circus potatoes straight to Frankenspud's house. Arnold Schwarzentater busted down the door. They marched through the house until they found Frankenspud. He was sitting in the kitchen eating dinner."

Matt motioned to Nick, and the big

boy sat down in a chair. Matt got the scrambled egg sandwich out of his backpack and handed it to Nick. Without even looking, Nick bit off half of the sandwich.

He chewed twice, and then his face turned to stone. The taste of the scrambled eggs was making him sick. Nick looked around, but there was no place to spit out the sandwich. He just sat there with a sick look on his face.

Matt continued reading. "The French Fry Brothers held Frankenspud while Potato Patty quickly wrapped a long vine around him."

Pulling a rope out of his pack, Matt quickly spun it around Nick. When Nick was tied tightly to the chair, Matt read on. "Reggie the Veggie took out his taterantula. Frankenspud shook with fear as Reggie held the spider in front of his face."

Matt reached into his pack and got a small box. Everyone gasped when he pulled out Harry, whose long legs wiggled in the air.

Matt held the spider in front of his Spud Bud. Nick's eyes were as big as basketballs. He was shaking so hard, the chair was bouncing up and down. Matt continued on with his story. "Tom Tater said to Frankenspud, 'Repeat after me: I will set all of my servants free. And I will never make another tater do anything he or she doesn't want to do ever again.' "

Matt whispered to Nick, "You better say it and mean it or I will put this spider on your head."

Nick closed his eyes tight. Swallowing the sandwich, he blurted out, "I set all of my servants free."

Matt let out a sigh of relief. He placed Harry back in the box and finished the story. "The tater tots cheered as they untied the big monster. And from then on Frankenspud and the tater tots were friends."

Matt untied Nick, who looked as if he had just seen a ghost. The room erupted in applause. Soon, everyone in both classes was congratulating the two boys on the best Tater Tale of the day.

Mrs. Pullman walked up to Nick. "Nicholas, I knew that you could do good work if you put your mind to it."

Mr. Broadhead shook Nick's hand. "Young man, you are quite an actor. You had me really believing that you were terrified of that spider."

Nick's face burst out into a smile. He leaned down and whispered to Matt, "You're not my servant anymore. From now on, you're just my Spud Bud."

It was the first *A* Nick had ever received on an assignment, and it seemed to have a nice effect on him. He even got a chance to read the school announcements over the intercom.

Nick took the opportunity to show how a real man burps. His blast blew out three speakers and caused Mrs. Johnson to faint.

About the Author

Gary Hogg has always loved stories and has been creating them since he was a boy growing up in Idaho.

Gary is also a very popular storyteller. Each year he brings his humorous tales to life for thousands of people around the United States.

He lives in Huntsville, Utah, with his wife, Sherry, and their children, Jackson, Jonah, Annie, and Boone.

LITTLE  APPLE®

Here are some of our favorite Little Apples.

There are fun times ahead with kids just like you in Little Apple books! Once you take a bite out of a Little Apple—you'll want to read more!

Reading Excitement for Kids with BIG Appetites!

☐ NA45899-X **Amber Brown Is Not a Crayon**
   Paula Danziger **$2.99**

☐ NA93425-2 **Amber Brown Goes Fourth**
   Paula Danziger **$2.99**

☐ NA50207-7 **You Can't Eat Your Chicken Pox, Amber Brown**
   Paula Danziger **$2.99**

☐ NA42833-0 **Catwings** Ursula K. LeGuin **$2.95**

☐ NA42832-2 **Catwings Return** Ursula K. LeGuin **$3.50**

☐ NA41821-1 **Class Clown** Johanna Hurwitz **$2.99**

☐ NA42400-9 **Five True Horse Stories**
   Margaret Davidson **$2.99**

☐ NA43868-9 **The Haunting of Grade Three**
   Grace Maccarone **$2.99**

☐ NA40966-2 **Rent a Third Grader** B.B. Hiller **$2.99**

☐ NA41944-7 **The Return of the Third Grade Ghost Hunters**
   Grace Maccarone **$2.99**

☐ NA42031-3 **Teacher's Pet** Johanna Hurwitz **$3.50**

Available wherever you buy books...or use the coupon below.

- -

SCHOLASTIC INC., P.O. Box 7502, 2931 East McCarty Street, Jefferson City, MO 65102

Please send me the books I have checked above. I am enclosing $ _____ (please add $2.00 to cover shipping and handling). Send check or money order—no cash or C.O.D.s please.

Name_____

Address_____

City_____State/Zip_____

Please allow four to six weeks for delivery. Offer good in the U.S.A. only. Sorry, mail orders are not available to residents of Canada. Prices subject to change.

LA996